This Little Tiger book
belongs to:

_____

_____

_____

To Len, who is not grumpy either (honest!)
~ S S

For Mel, who puts up with me when I'm grumpy and
makes me laugh when I need it most!
~ C P

LITTLE TIGER PRESS LTD,
an imprint of the Little Tiger Group
1 Coda Studios, 189 Munster Road, London SW6 6AW
www.littletiger.co.uk

First published in Great Britain 2019
This edition published 2020

A CIP catalogue record for this book is available from the British Library

Printed in China • LTP/1400/3055/1219

2 4 6 8 10 9 7 5 3 1

I'M NOT GRUMPY!

Steve Smallman • Caroline Pedler

LITTLE TIGER

LONDON

Mouse was in a particularly grumpy mood.
He'd woken up to find that the door to his oak tree
was blocked by A BIG FURRY BOTTOM!
"THAT'S JUST WHAT I NEED!" he grumbled,
climbing out of the window to see
what was going on.

Then, **splash**, a drop of water landed on Mouse's nose.
"RAIN!" he sighed. "THAT'S JUST WHAT I NEED!"

But it wasn't a raindrop.
It was a teardrop from a very sad little badger.

"WHERE'S MY MUMMY?" she wailed.
"I don't know!" squeaked Mouse.
"But I'll help you to find her if you
STOP THAT RACKET!"
Little Badger stopped crying.
Then, with a sniffle, she took
Mouse's paw and off they went.

They hadn't gone far when a butterfly fluttered past.
"PRETTY!" squealed Little Badger, galloping after it.
"STOP!" squeaked Mouse.

But when Little Badger did, Mouse was completely lost.
"THAT'S JUST WHAT I NEED," he groaned.

"Hello," said a squirrel-y voice,
"aren't you that grumpy mouse who lives in the old oak?"
"I AM NOT GRUMPY!" said Mouse grumpily.
"I am trying to get this little badger back to her mum."
"How kind!" said Squirrel. "My friend will know
where the Badgers live, come on!"

"Hello, Squirrel," hooted Owl.
"What a dear little badger! Oh, and you've brought lunch."
"I AM NOT LUNCH!" spluttered Mouse.
"Indeed," nodded Owl. "You're that grumpy mouse.
I don't eat grumpy mice, they're far too sour."
"Actually," said Squirrel, "he's trying to get
Little Badger home to her mum!"

"Then follow me," smiled Owl. "The forest is a dangerous place after dark so we'd better get going!"

Everyone followed Owl deeper
into the forest then,

splosh,

a drop of water landed on Mouse's nose.
"Oh, please don't start crying again!"
grumbled Mouse.

But it wasn't a teardrop,
it was a raindrop!

"THAT'S JUST WHAT I NEED!"
Mouse huffed as it started to pour.
"We must keep Little Badger dry," said Owl.
"Soggy badgers catch colds."
"Oh crumbs!" gasped Mouse.
"Anyone got an umbrella?"

"He's trying to get her home," said Squirrel quickly.
"What a kind friend!" smiled Bear.
Mouse blushed. He'd never been called a friend before.

"You're welcome to shelter under my tummy," said a big brown bear.
"But what is the grumpy mouse doing out here with Little Badger?"

When the rain stopped, Bear pointed them
in the right direction.
"And you'd better hurry," he said,
"it's getting late!"

On they trudged through
the darkening forest. Little Badger yawned.
"She's tired!" said Squirrel, as shadows
stretched across their path.
"Well, it's way past her bedtime,"
agreed Owl.

"I KNOW!" cried Mouse.
"She's TIRED, AND HUNGRY,
AND SCARED. AND SHE NEEDS HER MUM,
AND IT'S GETTING DARK, AND . . .
I don't know what to do!" he sobbed.

"There, there," said Squirrel.
Owl spread his wings. "I know what you need."
"HUG!" cheered Little Badger.

Mouse felt funny. Being a bit of a grumpy mouse,
he didn't get very many cuddles.

Suddenly, there was a flash of grey in the bushes.
"Mummy?" called Little Badger hopefully.
But it wasn't Mummy Badger. It was . . .

. . . a WOLF!
He swaggered over, licking his lips.

"Look what we have here!" the wolf sniggered.
"A squirrel for starters, a badger
and an owl for the main course,
and a mouse for pudding!"

"I AM NOT A PUDDING!"
shouted Mouse angrily.
"AND YOU CAN'T EAT MY FRIENDS!"
"Says who?" sneered the wolf.

"ME!"
shouted Mouse.

"AND ME!"
shouted Owl.

"AND ME!"
shouted Squirrel.

"AND ME!"

shouted Mummy Badger.

The wolf took one look at her angry eyes and scarpered.

Mummy Badger hugged Little Badger tight. "Thank you all for bringing her home!"

"It was Mouse's idea," said Squirrel.
"Well, thank you, Mr— wait a minute,"
said Mummy Badger. "Aren't you the grumpy mouse
who lives in the oak tree?"

"For the last time," huffed Mouse,
"I AM NOT GRUMPY . . . "

". . . at least, not anymore!"

And for the first time in a long time, Mouse smiled.

"Because now I have friends," he said.

"And friends, well, THAT'S JUST WHAT I NEED!"

Oh NO, BEAR!

JOANNE PARTIS

HIBERNATION HOTEL

John Kelly · Laura Brenlla

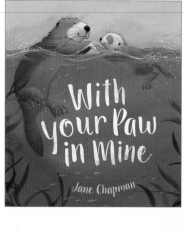

With your Paw in Mine

Jane Chapman

UNiCORN CLUB

SUZY SENIOR
LEIRE MARTÍN

More fun and friendship
with Little Tiger . . .

SUZANNE CHIEW · CAROLINE PEDLER

BADGER AND THE GREAT ADVENTURE

THE FIRST SLODGE

JEANNE WILLIS · JENNI DESMOND

LITTLE TIGER

For information regarding any of the above titles or for our catalogue, please contact us: Little Tiger Press Ltd, 1 Coda Studios, 189 Munster Road, London SW6 6AW • Tel: 020 7385 6333
E-mail: contact@littletiger.co.uk • www.littletiger.co.uk

First published 1988
by Walker Books Ltd
87 Vauxhall Walk
London SE11 5HJ

© 1988 Colin McNaughton

Reprinted 1989

Paperback edition published 1989

Printed in Italy by Grafedit S.p.A.

British Library Cataloguing in Publication Data
McNaughton, Colin
Santa Claus is Superman
I. Title
823'.914[J]   PZ7
ISBN 0-7445-1070-8
ISBN 0-7445-1327-8 (Pbk)